5-MINUTE MYSTERIES
FOR
MINECRAFTERS
THE CREEPER CODE

5-MINUTE MYSTERIES
FOR
MINECRAFTERS
THE CREEPER CODE

GREYSON MANN
ILLUSTRATED BY GRACE SANDFORD

Sky Pony Press
New York

Copyright © 2017 by Hollan Publishing, Inc.

Minecraft® is a registered trademark of Notch Development AB.

The Minecraft game is copyright © Mojang AB.

This book is not authorized or sponsored by Microsoft Corp., Mojang AB, Notch Development AB or Scholastic Inc., or any other person or entity owning or controlling rights in the Minecraft name, trademark, or copyrights.

Sky Pony Press books may be purchased in bulk at special discounts for sales promotion, corporate gifts, fund-raising, or educational purposes. Special editions can also be created to specifications. For details, contact the Special Sales Department, Sky Pony Press, 307 West 36th Street, 11th Floor, New York, NY 10018 or info@skyhorsepublishing.com.

Sky Pony® is a registered trademark of Skyhorse Publishing, Inc.®, a Delaware corporation.

Minecraft® is a registered trademark of Notch Development AB.
The Minecraft game is copyright © Mojang AB.

Visit our website at www.skyponypress.com.

10 9 8 7 6 5 4 3 2 1

Library of Congress Cataloging-in-Publication Data is available on file.

Special thanks to Erin L. Falligant.

Cover illustration by Grace Sandford
Cover design by Brian Peterson

Paperback ISBN: 978-1-5107-2369-6
Ebook ISBN: 978-1-5107-2371-9

Printed in Canada

5-MINUTE MYSTERIES

FOR

MINECRAFTERS

THE CREEPER CODE

CRACK THE CODES!

Ready to help Oliver, Audrey, and Sniffs solve a few mysteries in Birchtown? Many of these mysteries will ask you to solve a Creeper Code—to read secret messages hidden within a jumble of words. Here's how to crack those codes.

Read ONLY the words that come after the word "HISS."

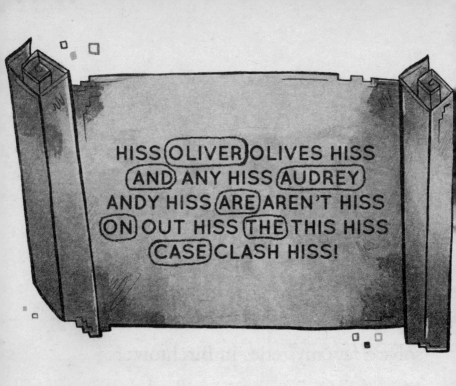

HISS (OLIVER) OLIVES HISS
(AND) ANY HISS (AUDREY)
ANDY HISS (ARE) AREN'T HISS
(ON) OUT HISS (THE) THIS HISS
(CASE) CLASH HISS!

BLOW-UP AT THE BLACKSMITH'S

"Check it out!" said Audrey, pointing toward the poster hanging in the window of the blacksmith's shop.

Oliver glanced at the poster, but he was distracted by his own reflection in the glass. He saw a boy with dark messy hair spilling into his glasses. And in those glasses, he saw another tiny reflection. He squinted, wondering how many Olivers he could see if he looked closely enough.

His big sister waved her hand in front of his face. "Did you read it or what?"

Oliver took a step backward and scanned the poster.

Audrey sighed. "Imagine what we could do with a *hundred* emeralds . . ."

Woof!

Oliver chuckled and bent low to scratch his gray dog behind the ears. "Sniffs knows *exactly* what he would do with a hundred emeralds. He'd buy a hundred bones."

Sniffs panted in agreement, his tongue hanging out as he smiled wide.

"Well, if I had a hundred emeralds, I'd buy a *diamond* sword today—not a boring old iron one," said Audrey. "C'mon. Let's find the blacksmith."

As she pushed through the heavy door, Oliver turned toward his dog. "Sit, Sniffs. Stay."

The dog whined, but he obediently lowered his rump to the ground.

"Good boy." Oliver pulled a worn skeleton bone from his pocket and gave it to Sniffs to gnaw on. Then he stepped into the shop.

Audrey was already deep in conversation with Blacksmith Bernard. "So about those creepers," she was saying.

"They've been showing up and *blowing* up all over Birchtown," said the blacksmith, his voice rising. "This morning, one spawned right here in my shop! You should see the damage."

He led Audrey and Oliver past the furnace room and into the back room. It was furnished with a simple bed on one side and a table on the other, just below a window.

Oliver's eyes slid past the tabby cat curled up on the table, past the teetering stack of books, and straight to the bowl of bright red apples on the window ledge. His mouth watered. Had he forgotten to have breakfast?

As he stepped into the room, something crunched under his feet. *Glass*. That's when he noticed that the window above the table was broken. A gentle breeze blew through.

"Luckily my walls are made of obsidian," said the blacksmith, opening the back door. "But you should see the crater in the ground."

Audrey stepped out first. "Woah!" The tips of her boots teetered on the edge of a gaping hole. "That must have been a mighty big creeper."

"Indeed," said the blacksmith with a sigh. "Now what did you say you came for? An iron sword? Let me run downstairs to my storage room and get one."

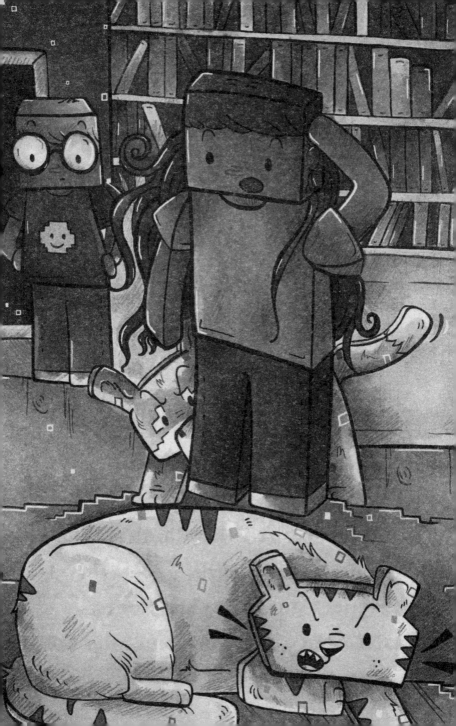

As soon as he was gone, Audrey pulled her old wooden sword from its sheath. She turned in a slow, steady circle, as if that enormous creeper was going to respawn any second now.

Oliver bent low to examine the crater. It was so deep! At the very bottom, he could see a few steps of a staircase.

"I don't think it was a creeper that did this damage," he said, straightening back up.

Audrey's face fell. "Why not?"

Why doesn't Oliver think a creeper was the culprit? Solve this Creeper Code for a clue. Read ONLY the words that come after the

word "BOOM." Then turn the page
to solve the mystery.

BOOM CREEPERS CLAPPERS BANG
BOOM RUN ROMP BOOM
AWAY AFAR BOOM FROM
FAST CLASH BOOM
CATS APPLES.

"I don't think it was creepers—for *two* reasons," said Oliver. "First, the blast must have come from outside the shop, because glass was on the floor *inside*."

Audrey chewed on a fingernail. "Okay. What else?"

"Creepers hate cats. A creeper wouldn't have blown up outside the window of a house where a cat was sleeping. That creeper would have turned and run the other away."

"So then what caused this?" asked Audrey, pointing toward the crater.

Oliver pushed up his glasses. "TNT, I'll bet. Maybe someone blew a hole to get to something valuable, like—"

"My emeralds!" cried the blacksmith, racing out the back door. "Someone broke into my storage chest! My emeralds are missing!"

Audrey sighed. "So much for the emerald reward."

But Oliver's eyes lit up. "Now we have *two* mysteries to solve," he said. "Why are so many creepers spawning in Birchtown? And who used TNT to steal Mr. Bernard's emeralds?"

Audrey pushed her shoulders back, standing tall. "Don't worry, Blacksmith Bernard. We're on the case. Right, Oliver?"

He gave her a thumbs-up. "Right."

From the front porch came a resounding *woof!*

WHEN SHADOWS FALL

Oliver shivered, pulling his cape tightly around him. "The sun is setting," he said, watching the orange globe sink behind the mountains.

Audrey glanced at the sky. "I know. Just one more house to visit before we call it a day."

She didn't seem the least bit worried about the mobs that might spawn in the dark. So, Oliver hurried to catch up to her. The closer he was to Audrey and her new iron sword, the safer he felt.

As soon as they reached the last house on the edge of Birchtown, the front door swung open. "Hi, kids," said red-headed Mrs. Tate. "Blacksmith Bernard said you might stop by, and I'm awfully glad to see you. We've had creepers in the house every night this week!" She glanced nervously at the setting sun.

"How do you think they're getting in?" asked Audrey as she stepped through the doorway.

Mrs. Tate shushed her with a finger. "The twins are sleeping." She nodded to two tiny beds at one end of the room.

"Oh, sorry!" Audrey clamped her hand over her mouth.

Oliver tiptoed past her and examined the room. He studied the front door, looked through each window, and snuck quietly past the sleeping twins.

Then he cleared his throat and whispered, "I don't think the creepers are getting in through a window or a door. I think they're spawning in here."

"How do you know?" asked Mrs. Tate, her eyes wide with worry.

Why does Oliver think the creepers are spawning in the room instead of getting in through a window or a door? Examine the room for clues. Then turn the page to solve the mystery.

Oliver pushed his glasses up on his nose. "Your door is solid. One window has a cactus in front of it. Creepers have trouble getting past those. The other window has cobwebs in it."

Mrs. Tate blushed. "I know. I've been meaning to clean, but . . ."

Audrey shrugged. "If I were you, I'd keep the cobwebs. Creepers get stuck in them!"

"Exactly," said Oliver. "So I think your problem is darkness. Creepers spawn in the shadows, and—"

Hisssssss . . .

Oliver whirled around to face the creeper. It stood at the foot of the children's beds!

Before Oliver could even gasp, Audrey sprang into action. She knocked the creeper back against the wall, again and again until it dissolved into a heap of gunpowder.

Mrs. Tate ran to her children, who were now wide-eyed and sitting up in bed. When the little boy began clapping and cheering, Audrey took a bow.

"Thank goodness you were here!" said Mrs. Tate.

"No, um, no problem," said Oliver, trying to keep his voice from shaking. "So maybe you could add a torch to that corner of the room."

But Mrs. Tate was already on it. She lifted a torch from above the furnace and slid it into the slot above the twins' beds. "It's just a nightlight," she said, tucking the children back into bed.

"No more creepers?" asked the little girl.

"No more creepers," said Mrs. Tate, kissing her on the forehead.

Disappointment flashed across the little boy's face, but Audrey gave him a thumbs-up, which made him smile.

"One creeper down," Audrey whispered to Oliver on their way out the door. "Only like a gazillion more to go."

MUSIC FROM THE WELL

Sniffs cocked his furry head and whined.

"He hears the music too!" said Oliver. "But where's it coming from?" He held his torch higher, trying to see.

Audrey leaned over the edge of the Birchtown well. "From down here, just like the villagers said!" Her voice bounced off the cobblestone walls.

"But how?" asked Oliver. Examining clues on the ground was one thing. Solving a mystery deep within the depths of a well was another.

Then he caught sight of the bucket on the rope. *Audrey had better not ask me to—*

"Lower me down, Oliver," she said, reaching for the bucket.

"No. It's dangerous!" he argued. But *danger* was practically Audrey's middle name.

"You think everything is dangerous," she said. "Like being outside at night. But so far, we haven't been attacked by any hostile mobs, right?"

Oliver shivered. "Don't remind me. Why did we have to do this at night again?"

Audrey rolled her eyes. "Because the villagers hear the music at night. You want to solve the mystery, right? So, hand me that torch and lower me down."

As she climbed into the bucket, Oliver took a deep breath and reached for the rope.

Creak, creak, creak . . .

He dug his heels into the earth and slowly lowered his sister down.

Splash! The bucket finally hit water. Then there was silence.

"Audrey?" Oliver fought the panic rising in his chest.

"I'm fine." Her voice sounded very far away. "I can still hear the music, even louder now. But it's not coming from down here. There's not a jukebox or music disc in sight. Okay, bring me back up!"

Oliver tugged on the rope. Bringing his sister up was much harder than lowering her down. Even Sniffs tried to help.

Finally, Audrey's head popped up out of the well. As she climbed out of the bucket, Oliver tied off the rope and wiped the sweat from his forehead.

"The music must be coming from underground," said Audrey. "Maybe from a basement?"

Oliver pushed up his glasses and gazed left, then right. The well stood halfway between the Birchtown library and the clock tower. The clock tower *bonged* every hour, but Oliver had never heard music coming from the tower.

Suddenly, Sniffs growled. He crouched low, ready to spring at something in the darkness.

Audrey snapped into ready position. She pulled her sword from her side. "Skeletons!"

Then Oliver heard it, too: the rattling of bones. "Where are they?"

"I don't know," said Audrey. "But without a bow and arrow, we're goners. I'll never get close enough to a skeleton to use my sword—not without armor!"

Fear exploded in Oliver's chest. If Audrey was scared, they *were* goners. He didn't have any weapons at all.

When Sniffs barked and leaped into the shadows, Oliver grabbed his sister's arm.

Then they heard something else—the creak of the front door to the library. "Oliver! Audrey! Get in here!" called Librarian Lila. She waved the kids inside.

Oliver tripped up the stairs. He could hardly wait to get through that door! Then he saw that the librarian carried a bow and arrow. As they headed in, she was heading out—to fight.

"I'm going with you!" said Audrey. "I'll help."

The librarian shook her head. "Stay here."

So Audrey and Oliver watched through a crack in the door. The librarian raced down the steps, darted behind the well, and carefully aimed her bow. *Thwang!* She shot an arrow into the darkness.

When an arrow whizzed back, she ducked. Then she fired another arrow behind her, in the opposite direction.

"She's surrounded!" cried Audrey.

Oliver scrunched his eyes tight.

"Wait, I see what she's doing," said Audrey a moment later. "She's making the skeletons fight each other!"

Sure enough, as Librarian Lila raced back up the steps, bows whizzed back and forth behind her. Oliver heard a

grunt and a groan, and then the tinkle
of bones hitting the ground.

Just as the librarian began to
close the door, a furry snout poked
through. "Sniffs!" Oliver dropped to
his knees. He laughed when he saw

the fresh skeleton bone in the dog's mouth. "You claimed a treasure."

"And I think I solved the mystery of the music from the well," said Audrey, grinning.

"Wait, really?" Oliver glanced up.

"Yup," said Audrey. Then she turned to the librarian. "You don't by chance have a jukebox in your basement, do you?"

Why does Audrey think Librarian Lila is playing the mysterious music? Solve this Creeper Code for a clue. Read ONLY the words that come after the word "GREEN." Then turn the page to solve the mystery.

GREEN CREEPERS CLAPPERS GRAY
GREEN DROP DRIP GREEN MUSIC
GRAND GREEN DISCS DART GRIP
GREEN WHEN GRASS GREEN
STRUCK GROW GREEN BY GREEN
SKELETON SCARY GREEN ARROWS.

Librarian Lila blushed in the glow of the torch. "You caught me. I was hoping no one would hear the music!"

"But how did you figure it out?" asked Oliver, staring at Audrey in amazement.

She shrugged. "Easy. How do you get music discs?"

He thought about that. "You get a skeleton to shoot a creeper."

"Right," said Audrey. "Did you see what Librarian Lila did out there? She got the skeletons to shoot *each other*. Getting them to shoot a creeper would be easy for her!"

The librarian chuckled. "Well, it's never easy. But I've definitely added a few music discs to my collection lately."

"Wait," said Oliver. "Why didn't you want anyone else to hear the music?"

The librarian shrugged. "Villagers are so upset by all the creepers in town. I might be the only one who thinks something *good* can come from a creeper! You won't tell anyone, will you?"

Audrey pretended to zip her lips with her fingers. "Your secret is safe with us—as long as you teach me how to use a bow and arrow like that someday."

The librarian smiled. "Deal."

WHATEVER THE WEATHER

As Oliver passed the front door of the butcher's shop, he heard loud voices escape from inside.

"What in the Overworld is going on in there?" he asked.

"Let's find out," said Audrey, veering in her path.

Oliver hung back for a moment beside Sniffs, who was lapping water from a puddle. Then he sighed and followed his sister up the steps.

As she pushed through the front door, the angry voices swelled.

"I know it was you!" shouted Farmer Fran, pointing her finger at Butcher Bart. "You blew up my shed last night. I saw you outside in the rain!"

The butcher held up his gloved hands. "It wasn't me. I was outside last night, yes—tracking a zombie pigman. But I most certainly didn't blow up your shed. Why would I do that?"

"I don't know. To get at my pigs maybe?" said the farmer. "Or maybe you're just a dirty griefer."

Uh-oh, thought Oliver. *This is going from bad to worse.*

He inched back toward the door, but Audrey held up her hand. "Excuse me," she said. "Do you mind if Oliver and I take a look at the scene of this crime?"

"Be my guest," said Farmer Fran, spreading her arms wide. "It'll only prove my case!"

A few minutes later, they stood by what used to be the farmer's shed, just on the edge of Birchtown. Sniffs had his nose to the ground, exploring the edges of the blown-out crater.

"See?" said Farmer Fran. "Judging by the size of that hole, it *had* to be a griefer using TNT."

Butcher Bart shook his head. "That's a creeper explosion. I didn't cause that."

"Let's examine the evidence," said Oliver. His voice wasn't nearly as loud and confident as Audrey's. But he was surprised when the farmer and the butcher stopped arguing. They stepped aside, letting him explore the property.

The crater *was* quite deep. As Oliver stepped around it and over a downed tree branch, he glanced at the oak tree above. The tree was practically split in half. Part of the jagged trunk was still standing, but its edges were burned black.

When Oliver lifted the fallen branch to examine the wet ground below, he spotted something white and glistening—something *grinning* at him. A skeleton's skull!

"Um, Audrey?" he called, his voice quivering. His sister knew way more about skeletons than he did.

When she hurried over to take a look, Oliver whispered something in her ear. She nodded and whispered something back.

By then, Farmer Fran and Butcher Bart were arguing again. So Audrey put two fingers in her mouth and whistled to get their attention.

"Oliver and I have cracked the case," she announced. "And this time, the culprit was definitely a creeper."

"How do you know?" asked Farmer Fran, her voice still hot with anger.

How does Oliver know a creeper caused the explosion? Solve this Creeper Code for a clue. Read ONLY the words that come after the word "HISS." Then turn the page to solve the mystery.

HISS CREEPERS CLAPPERS HAVE HISS
HIT HAPPENED HOT HISS BY THIS
HISS LIGHTNING THUNDER
HISS BECOME BETTER BITERS
HISS SUPER SAPPY
HISS CHARGED CHANGED.

Oliver cleared his throat. "Judging by this tree, there was a lightning storm last night. When lightning strikes a pig, it turns into a zombie pigman."

"Yes! That's what I saw last night!" said Butcher Bart.

"But do you know what happens when lightning strikes a creeper?" Audrey chimed in.

Farmer Fran's face relaxed. "They become super charged," she said with a sigh.

"Right," said Oliver. "The final clue was the skeleton's skull. When a skeleton is killed by a charged creeper, it kind of, well, loses its head." He grinned.

Farmer Fran smiled. "I kind of lost my head, too," she said. "Sorry Bart. My mistake." She reached out to shake the butcher's hand.

"No worries," said Butcher Bart. "Whatever the weather, we've got a creeper problem in Birchtown."

"A *super*-charged creeper problem," said Audrey, laughing. "But never fear. My super-smart brother and I are on the case. Right, Oliver?"

This time Oliver's voice was loud and clear. "Right!"

SKETCHING A SUSPECT

"I'm armed and ready," said Audrey, sliding her sword into its sheath.

"Me, too," said Oliver, patting his notebook.

Audrey did a double take. "What are you going to do with that old thing?" she asked.

He shrugged. "Every good detective needs a notebook, right?"

He had found
the book at the
bottom of his chest
just this morning.
There were only a
few tattered pages
inside, and the
leather cover was so worn that Sniffs
eyed it up as if it were a chew toy.

"Hands off," said Oliver in his most
stern voice. "I mean, *mouth* off. No
slobbering on my book, Sniffs. It's for
very important business."

The dog whined and went back to
sniffing the ground.

"Which way to Lefty's place?" asked
Audrey, stopping by a signpost.

Oliver pushed up his glasses. "Take a right," he said, jogging to catch up with his sister. They followed the short gravel path toward the leatherworker's house.

Lefty greeted them on the porch. "Hey, kids! Are you here to help me catch the creeper that's been lurking around my yard?"

"Yes!" said Audrey. "Show us those footprints we've been hearing about."

"Okay," said Lefty, looking in both directions. "But keep an eye out. Those creepers are way too sneaky."

He led them beside a tall fence and then knelt in the dirt. "I caught a glimpse of the mob through the fence.

You can just barely make out the prints. They're still pretty fresh."

Sniffs stuck his nose right into one of the footprints. When Audrey saw the direction the prints were heading, she took off like a shot. And Oliver? He hung back and sketched the prints in his notebook.

"So," he said, clearing his throat. "You say you saw this creeper. About how tall would you say he was?"

Lefty scratched his chin. "I don't know. I guess, about . . . you know, Steve's height." He waved at his neighbor Steve, who was digging in his garden.

"Uh-huh, uh-huh," said Oliver, jotting notes in his notebook. "And what color would you say he was?"

Lefty snorted. "Well, *green,* of course."

"Right," said Oliver, jotting that down. "Got it. And was the mob making any sounds?"

"Nope. Well, hissing probably. I'm not sure. I couldn't hear anything through my kitchen window."

Oliver studied his notes. "Hmm. Okay, just one more question, Lefty. Would you say this mob was right-handed or left-handed?"

Lefty slapped his thigh and laughed out loud. "Kid, you crack me up. How should I know? The creeper had both arms in the air. That's about all I can say."

As Audrey circled back toward them, Oliver closed his notebook.

"Are you going to help me look for the creeper or what?" asked Audrey, hands in the air.

Oliver squinted up into the morning sun. "He's long gone," he said.

"How do you know?" asked Audrey. "Creepers don't burn up at dawn."

"No . . ." said Oliver slowly. "But this is no creeper we're tracking."

How can Oliver be so sure? Solve this Creeper Code for a clue. Read ONLY the words that come after the word "MOB." Then turn the page to solve the mystery.

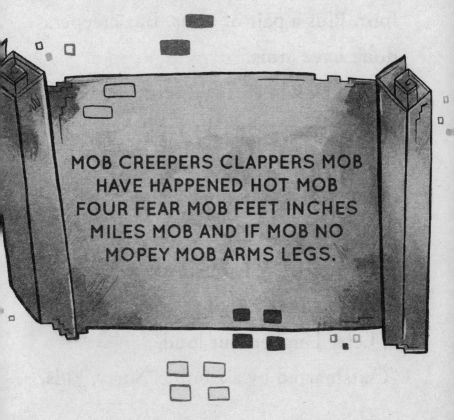

MOB CREEPERS CLAPPERS MOB
HAVE HAPPENED HOT MOB
FOUR FEAR MOB FEET INCHES
MILES MOB AND IF MOB NO
MOPEY MOB ARMS LEGS.

"But Lefty saw a creeper," Audrey argued. "He told us! He showed us the footprints, too."

"Right," said Oliver. "But the mob that left those prints had two feet, not four. Plus a pair of arms. But creepers don't have arms."

"Well, I'll be . . ." said Lefty. "So what's been lurking around my yard, then?"

Oliver held up the sketch he had drawn in his notebook.

"About Steve's height, with two legs and outstretched arms. And very green. Does this look like the suspect?"

Lefty laughed out loud.

"Outsmarted by a zombie. Sorry, kids,

for dragging you all the way out here for nothing."

"Oh, it wasn't for nothing," said Oliver, grinning. "I finally got to use my notebook. And I think it's going to come in pretty *handy*!"

"WITCH" POTION WAS IT?

"No, Sniffs! You spit that out right now. Drop it."

Oliver pointed his finger until the guilty dog opened his mouth. A mini slime dropped out.

Oinga, boing, oinga, boing . . .

As the tiny mob bounced toward the swamp, Sniffs licked at the slime oozing from his snout.

"Gross!" said Oliver. "No more kisses from you today. You can keep all that slimy goodness to yourself."

Sniffs wagged his tail and took off toward Audrey, who was peering at something on the mushy, wet ground. "Here it is!" she called, waving Oliver over. "Gunpowder everywhere. There was a creeper battle here for sure."

While she searched the edge of the oak grove for more mobs, Oliver examined the gunpowder. Something wet and glistening lay on the grass beside it. *A mushroom?*

Sniffs spotted it, too—he was a big fan of mushrooms. But as his jaws clamped down on the squishy something, Oliver sprang into action. "Drop it, Sniffs. Now!"

Sniffs did, and the gooey brown spider eye dropped to the ground.

"That's no mushroom," said Oliver. "That'll make you sick."

He used a stick to poke at the eyeball. Then a thought struck. "Audrey!" he cried, jumping up. "There wasn't a *creeper* battle here. Someone battled a . . . hey, watch out!"

Audrey saw the witch at the same time Oliver did. She whirled around to face the purple-robed mob.

The witch was already downing a potion from her glass bottle.

Before she could finish the powerful liquid, Audrey attacked. She struck the witch with her sword, dodging splash potions as she backed the witch up toward the water.

Finally the witch fell, and her glass bottle did, too. It hit a rock and crashed into a million tiny shards.

"No!" cried Audrey, dropping to her knees. "I wanted that potion for myself!"

Oliver ran toward her and helped her up. "Would you settle for a spider eye?" he asked, pointing toward the fresh drop lying where the witch used to be.

Audrey shivered. "Uh, no thanks." She kept her sword raised as she looked out over the swamp. "There must be a witch hut around here somewhere. There!"

The wooden house was built on stilts. A couple of loose boards dangled from the porch, and the front door hung crooked on its hinges.

"Did someone destroy the hut to get to the witch?" asked Oliver.

"Maybe. Or to get to the witch's *potions*," Audrey said, her eyes narrowed. "Let's go check it out!"

Every inch of Oliver wanted to walk the other way. But somehow, he found himself standing beside Audrey inside the witch hut. It was empty, thank goodness. And there were a couple of empty spots on the shelf above the cauldron, too.

Audrey pointed. "Someone stole some potion ingredients. See?"

Before Oliver could jot down the missing ingredients in his notebook, Sniffs nosed at his hand.

"What, boy?"

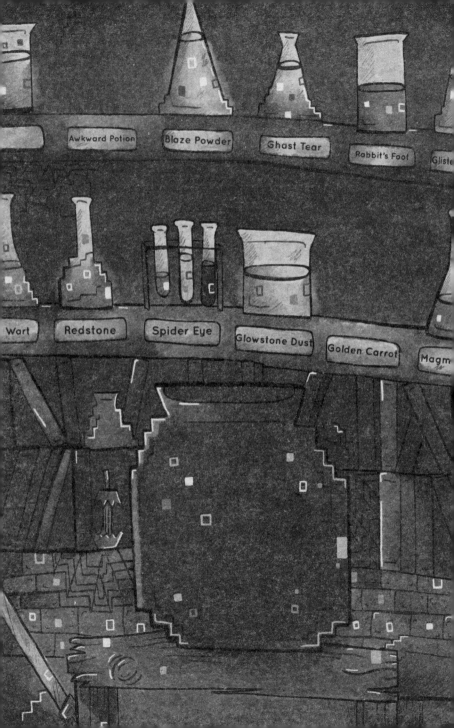

The dogs' ears perked up, as if to say, "Listen!"

Then Oliver heard it, too. *Squish, slop, squish, slop, squish, slop* . . . The sound grew louder.

"Audrey, I think we're about to get slimed."

Her eyes widened. She grabbed a book off the shelf and headed for the door. "Let's go!"

There was nothing "mini" about the slimes at the base of the ladder. Audrey struck the first one with her sword, breaking it into a gazillion smaller slimes. "Run!" she shouted to Oliver.

She didn't have to tell him twice. He sprinted down the mucky trail toward home, with Sniffs by his side.

An hour later, he and Audrey huddled under a torch looking at the book she had taken from the hut.

"Two ingredients were stolen," she said. "One was awkward potion. Do you remember the other one?"

Awkward Potion +
Glistering Melon =
Potion of Healing
Awkward Potion
+ Rabbit's Foot
= Potion of Leaping

Awkward Potion
+ Golden Carrot
= Potion of Night Vision
Awkward Potion
+ Spider Eye
= Potion of Poison

Do you remember the other stolen ingredient? Which potion is the thief trying to make? Take a guess, and then turn the page to solve the mystery.

Oliver scrunched his eyes shut, trying to remember. "I think it was Golden Carrot," he finally said. "And if it was, then someone was trying to make . . ." He slid his finger along the chart in Audrey's book.

"Potion of night vision!" she announced. "That means someone has plans to do something mysterious in the dark."

"But who?" added Oliver. "And what?"

Sniffs, who was settled beside him, let out a low growl.

"Easy boy," said Oliver. "We figured out which potion ingredients were stolen and why. We'll figure out the *next* mystery, too."

TRAPPED IN A LIE

Bong, bong, bong . . .

The bell in the clock tower rang a few more times and then settled into silence.

"How many was that, Sniffs? Nine times?" Oliver shaded his eyes and scanned the horizon. Where was Audrey? She'd been visiting villagers all morning but was supposed to be here at 8:30—a half hour ago.

While he waited, Oliver watched an iron golem roam the courtyard, offering poppies to villagers. Other villagers traded with one another, calling out their wares.

Farmer Fran traded apples from her cart to a shepherd for some sheared wool. Miner Max offered gunpowder to Lefty in exchange for some leather armor. When Max offered more gunpowder to a fisherman for freshly caught salmon, Sniff's nose twitched.

"That's not for you, boy," said Oliver. "Not unless you have something to trade for it. Do you?"

Sniffs cocked his head, as if he were thinking about it. Then he whined and laid down on his belly, resting his chin on his paws.

"Hey! Sorry I'm late," huffed Audrey. She jogged toward them through the crowd. "You'll never believe how many villagers saw creepers this morning. They said a whole *army* of the green mobs passed by town! It was like someone had a room full of them and then opened the door and just let them out."

"You mean like a creeper trap?" asked Oliver.

Audrey shrugged. "Maybe. But who would want to trap a bunch of dirty creepers?"

Oliver pushed up his glasses and scanned the courtyard. "Someone who wants a lot of gunpowder."

Audrey's eyes widened. "Like someone making TNT?" she whispered. "But who?"

Oliver watched Miner Max walk away from the fisherman's cart. He was limping a little.

"Max sure had a lot of gunpowder to trade this morning," Oliver whispered to Audrey. "Should we question him?"

She nodded. "I'm on it."

A few minutes later, they were talking with Max in front of his obsidian mine. "Yeah, I saw those creepers this morning," he said. "Someone must have trapped them—one of my neighbors. In fact, I saw a warning painted on a sign yesterday afternoon." He waved his arm and said, "Follow me. I'll show you."

The warning was written in red paint on a simple wooden signpost. It read:

BEWARE.
CREEPERS ON THE
LOOSE!

"I don't know who wrote it," said Max, shrugging. "I'm just glad the creepers have cleared out."

Audrey didn't seem so sure the creepers were gone. She kept her hand on her sword.

Oliver sketched the sign into his notebook. Then he crouched beside the sign, searching for clues. He looked under and around it. Sniffs did, too.

As the dog's nose brushed against the sign, a streak of red paint smeared across his snout.

"Oh, no! Sniffs, come here," said Oliver. He tried to wipe off the paint, but poor Sniffs looked like he had just battled a hostile mob.

Then another thought struck.

"Miner Max, how did you hurt your leg?" Oliver called to the miner, who was limping up ahead.

"What? Oh, um, I fell into a ravine while I was mining. It's no big deal."

"Oh, okay."

Something in Max's voice caught Audrey's attention. She fell into step beside him and whispered, "Do you know who built the creeper trap?"

Oliver nodded. "Max did," he mouthed.

Why is Oliver so sure? Solve this Creeper Code for a clue. Read ONLY the words that come after the word "CREEP." Then turn the page to solve the mystery.

CREEP MAX MIX CREEP LIED LAID.
CREEP THE THIS CREEP SIGN SAME
CREEP WAS WASTE CREEP PAINTED
PRINTED CREEP TODAY TONIGHT
CREEP NOT KNIT CREEP
YESTERDAY YARN

Audrey cleared her throat. "Miner Max, are you sure there's nothing you want to tell us about a creeper trap?"

The miner's face fell. "You kids are on to me, aren't you?"

Oliver nodded. "It was the wet paint on the sign that gave it away. You couldn't have seen it yesterday afternoon—it wasn't made yet. Did you make the sign, Miner Max?"

The miner sighed. "I built the creeper trap a week ago to collect more gunpowder. I need TNT for mining obsidian! But creepers kept slipping out. One exploded on the other side of the trap door this morning. That's how I hurt my leg. And before I could fix

the door, every last creeper crept out!"
He hung his head.

Audrey's eyes lit up. "Well that
explains the creeper problem in
Birchtown. One mystery solved."

Miner Max nodded sadly. "I'll
go back into town and let the other
villagers know."

Oliver felt a little sorry for the
miner as he limped back toward town.
"Should we go with him?" he asked.

Audrey nibbled on a fingernail.
"Not yet," she said. "Do you think
Max really used the TNT for mining?
Someone used TNT to blow a hole
into the blacksmith's storage room and
steal his emeralds, remember?"

Oliver shook his head. "Max didn't steal any emeralds."

"How do you know?" she asked.

"Because," said Oliver. "If Max stole the emeralds, he would have been trading with them at the market this morning. You can buy a lot more with emeralds than you can with gunpowder!"

Audrey's face relaxed into a smile. "So the miner was telling the truth after all. Should we help him go tell the villagers what happened?"

Woof! said Sniffs.

Oliver laughed and followed his dog *back* down the gravel road toward Miner Max—and Birchtown.

SWAMP SECRETS

"It's your turn to take out the trash," Audrey insisted. "I did it last week!"

Oliver sighed and grabbed the trash can. In the time it would take to win this argument, he could make it to the lava pit and back again.

"C'mon, Sniffs," he called as he headed out the door.

The lava pit just outside of Birchtown glowed bright. Oliver waved at Lefty, who had just emptied his own bin.

"Sit, Sniffs," said Oliver. "Don't get too close to the flames."

The dog obeyed. But as Oliver poured his trash into the bubbling lava, the breeze lifted a piece of half-burned paper out of the pit. And then another. And another.

Sniffs saw them, too. He barked and chased the paper scraps.

By the time Oliver pried them out of the dog's mouth, they were not only half-burned, but half-chewed, too.

He knelt down and laid out the scraps on the grass.

"What did you find?" called
Audrey, coming up behind Oliver.

"A map, I think," he said. "Take a look."

She studied the scraps. "Yeah, that
does look like a map. This blue blob is

water, and here are some trees. Look, someone marked an X by one of them! That's mysterious."

Oliver pushed up his glasses. "Buried treasure, you think?" he asked, half-kidding.

Audrey's eyes danced. "Buried *emeralds*, maybe! But where is this place?"

Oliver squinted and studied the squiggles on the map.

"Are these lily pads?" He pointed.

"Yes!" said Audrey. "So this must be a map of the swamp. Maybe the emeralds are buried there!"

She looked so excited, Oliver feared she'd take off for the swamp without him. "Let me bring the trash can home and get my notebook," he said. "Then we'll go together, okay?"

Fifteen minutes later, they were trudging through the swamp. Oliver hoped they wouldn't run into any witches—or squishy eyeballs—like they had the last time they were here.

After crossing a lily pad bridge and circling every tree, they hadn't run into any mobs. But they hadn't found buried treasure either.

"There's a whole *grove* of oak trees here. How are we supposed to find the one with the X by it?" grumbled Audrey.

Oliver raised his hands at his sides—and a scrap of map slipped out of his notebook and fluttered to the ground. As he bent to pick it up, he noticed a word scribbled on the back: *ROOMS*.

When he flipped over the other two scraps, he saw two more words. "*Brown? Mush?* What do these words mean?"

He tried rearranging the scraps until they made *two* words instead of three. Audrey watched over his shoulder.

"Oh!" she said. "I get it."

Can you rearrange these three words into just two? Give it a try, and then turn the page.

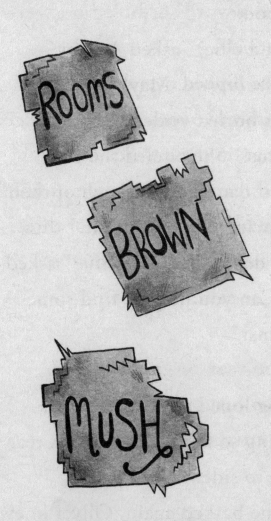

Max copied the new words into his notebook.

"Is that a clue?" asked Audrey. "*Brown mushrooms*. Maybe the treasure is buried under a patch of mushrooms!" She circled the trees again, as if dancing with each of them before moving on to the next.

"What do you think, Sniffs?" asked Oliver. "Can you help us find some mushrooms?"

Woof!

The dog loped after Audrey, his tail wagging so hard it moved his rear from side to side.

When he barked again, Oliver knew the dog had found something special.

He raced toward Sniffs, who was digging at the base of a large oak. Brown mushrooms popped out of the moist earth, but Sniffs was interested in something else. He dug deeper, black dirt spraying out behind him onto Audrey's boots.

Then Oliver heard the dog's claws scratch wood. "He found something! C'mon, Sniffs. Let us see, too."

He pulled Sniffs back and reached into the hole, dusting the dirt off the top of a wooden box. A wooden *chest*.

Audrey helped him dig it out of the hole. Then they counted to three and opened it together.

"Emeralds!" shouted Audrey.

Oliver sucked in his breath. He could barely believe it!

"We found buried treasure!" said Audrey, running her fingers through the smooth green stones. "The map led us right to them."

"Well, *Sniffs* led us right to them," laughed Oliver, giving his dog a thank-you scratch behind the ear. "But now we have a new mystery to solve."

"Who buried the emeralds?" said Audrey.

"Exactly," said Oliver. "Every time we solve one mystery, another one comes along." But he didn't sound the *least* bit disappointed.

BY GOLEM, WE GOT 'IM

"Ar-roooo!"

Oliver sat up with a start in the dark room. "Sniffs?"

The dog howled again and then scratched urgently at the front door.

"Okay, okay, I'm coming." Oliver pulled back his blanket and slid out of bed. He crossed the chilly floor with his bare feet and unlocked the front door.

As soon as the door opened, Sniffs pushed through it and took off like a shot into the dark night.

"Sniffs! Come back!"

Audrey padded across the floor behind Oliver, rubbing her eyes. "What time is it?"

"Late. Or early. Like middle-of-the-night early." Oliver checked the clock, which read 3:15.

"Where's that crazy dog going?"

Oliver shrugged. "Chasing a mob maybe." He yawned and started back toward his bed, until another howl and a pitiful yelp stopped him in his tracks. "Sniffs!"

Oliver raced out of the house in his bare feet, with Audrey close behind him. Sharp rocks littered the gravel path toward town, but he didn't care. He had to get to his dog!

"I can't see!" cried Audrey. "It's so dark!"

A cluster of torches soon lit their way. Villagers were gathered on the edge of town.

But why? wondered Oliver. He ran faster—and suddenly tripped over something hard and heavy.

"Is that a brick?" asked Audrey, helping him up.

Oliver rubbed his stubbed toes and squinted into the darkness. "No, it looks like an iron ingot."

"Uh-oh. Did something happen to Birchtown's iron golem?" Audrey raced ahead toward the crowd.

When Oliver caught up, he tried to make sense of the chaos. A gaping crater had appeared in the middle of the courtyard. Iron ingots and poppies littered the ground. A rumpled traveler sat on the ground, his face covered in soot. And a ring of villagers—plus one growling dog— stood just a few feet away.

"Sniffs!" Oliver ran to his dog. "What happened to you? What's going on?"

"That's what we'd like to know," said Blacksmith Bernard. He stood, arms crossed, facing the man on the ground. "What did you say your name was again?"

"Levi," said the man, pushing himself up. He extended his hand, but Bernard didn't take it. "I was

enjoying a perfectly peaceful night walk, admiring the moon, when a creeper snuck up behind me. Then, BAM! Your iron golem was there to defend me.  He fought hard against the creeper, but as you can see, that dirty mob blew him to bits!"

Librarian Lucy stepped forward, holding her torch. "Iron golems don't attack creepers," she said simply.

Boy, she sure knows a lot about fighting, thought Oliver.

Levi shrugged. "Then I guess that golem was attacking this vicious dog here, and the creeper got caught in the cross-fire."

Sniffs growled, and hot anger swelled in Oliver's chest. "Iron golems don't attack dogs," he said, stepping in front of Sniffs. "I think the golem was attacking *you*."

"Oliver!" said Audrey in surprise. "Why do you think that?"

He tried to keep his voice from shaking. "Because I caught him in a lie."

What lie did Oliver catch Levi telling? Solve this Creeper Code for a clue. Read ONLY the words that come after the word "BLAST." Then turn the page to solve the mystery.

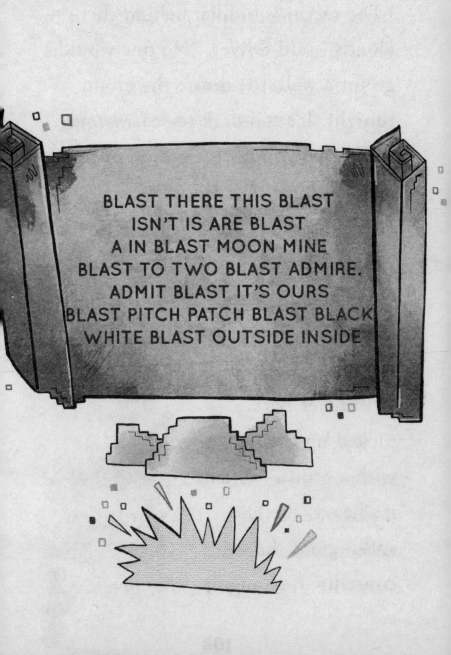

"The moon is hidden behind the clouds," said Oliver. "No one would go for a walk to admire the moon tonight. It's too dark to see *anything*."

"Unless you have a potion of night vision!" Audrey piped up.

Levi shook his head. "If I'm lying about the moon and the creeper, then what do you think caused this explosion?"

"TNT," announced Blacksmith Bernard. "Let's check his bag."

Butcher Bart picked up the sack with a grunt. "Woah, it's heavy," he said, spilling out the contents. Iron ingots

plunked out into a teetering pile, along with a flint and steel.

"You blew up our iron golem with TNT to get ingots!" accused one villager.

"To trade for emeralds," said another, shaking her fist. "You dirty griefer."

"Wait, that's not all," said Oliver, noticing a bump in the bottom of the sack. He dug down deep and pulled out a bottle made of thick glass. Orange liquid sloshed inside.

"Potion?" asked Librarian Lila. "Which one?"

"Potion of night vision!" said Audrey. "I *knew* it."

"Mystery solved," said Blacksmith Bernard. "Let's get this thief into a jail cell so that we can all get some more sleep before dawn. We have some rebuilding to do tomorrow."

"C'mon, Sniffs," said Oliver. "You did your job, buddy. Let's go home."

As they hurried out of town, the clouds parted for a split second—just long enough for the moon to cast a glow over Birchtown, and long enough for Oliver to grin at his big sister.

"We did it!" he said. "Mysteries solved."

"All of them," she said, her eyes dancing. "At least for now."

MYSTERY GIFTS

"They're here!" announced Librarian Lila from the doorway. She waved the kids inside.

Oliver was surprised to see the blacksmith and the butcher standing behind her. And on a long wooden library table, he spotted three brightly wrapped gifts.

"They're not emeralds," said Blacksmith Bernard. "But we wanted to reward you kids for your work in cracking the mysteries in Birchtown. We picked out something special for each one of you."

He handed Audrey a package wrapped in glittery blue paper. Oliver's was wrapped in green-striped paper.

"And this one is for Sniffs," said Butcher Bart. "Wait, where's Sniffs?"

When paws scrabbled outside the door, the librarian laughed and let the poor dog in.

"That's better, isn't it, Sniffs?" she said. "Do you want your present now?"

Woof! He nosed at the gift in her hand.

"Wait!" said the blacksmith. "Don't you kids want to guess what we got you? We'll give you a clue." He tapped his chin and then said, "Every gift starts with the letters **B** and **O**."

What did each "detective" receive as a gift? Take a guess, and then turn the page to find out.

Audrey got a B O __

Oliver got a B O __ __

Sniffs for a B O __ __.

Before Oliver could take a guess, Sniffs had already chewed open his gift—a tasty new bone!

"Sniffs! You were supposed to guess," teased Oliver. "But maybe your nose knew what was inside."

When he heard the sound of paper ripping, Oliver whirled around. Audrey had torn open her gift, too! She held a beautiful new bow and arrow.

"Do you like it?" asked Librarian Lila. "I picked it out myself."

Audrey ran her finger along the smooth bow. "I don't just like it," she said. "I *love* it!"

"But you were supposed to guess!" said Oliver, trying not to whine.

Audrey shrugged. "I think we've solved enough mysteries lately, don't you? Open yours now, Oliver!"

He sighed and peeled back a piece of the wrapping paper. When he saw the smooth leather cover beneath, he tore off the rest of the paper in one fell swoop. "A new notebook!" He raised the leather cover to his nose and took a big sniff. Then he opened the book and flipped through the crisp white pages.

"Now you can take more notes," said Audrey with a smile.

"And solve more mysteries," said Oliver, hugging the book to his chest. "I can't wait to get started!"

"Me neither," said Audrey, sliding an arrow into her bow. "How about you down there, Bone Breath?"

Woof!

THE END

CREEPER CODE ANSWER KEY:

Blow-Up at the Blacksmith's
Answer: Creepers run away from cats.

Music From the Wall
Answer: Creepers drop music discs when
struck by skeleton arrows.

Whatever the Weather
Answer: Creepers hit by lightning become
super charged.

Sketching a Suspect
Answer: Creepers have four feet and no arms.

Trapped in a Lie
Answer: Max lied. The sign was painted
today, not yesterday.

By Golem, We Got 'im
Answer: There's no moon to admire. It's
pitch black outside!